Usborne
10 Ten-Minute
Fairy Tales

Usborne
10 Ten-Minute
Fairy Tales

Designed by Laura Nelson Norris

CONTENTS

LITTLE RED RIDING HOOD   6

By the Brothers Grimm, retold by Rob Lloyd Jones
Illustrated by Lorena Alvarez

THE ELVES AND THE SHOEMAKER   32

By the Brothers Grimm, retold by Rob Lloyd Jones
Illustrated by John Joven

THE EMPEROR AND THE NIGHTINGALE   56

By Hans Christian Andersen, retold by Rosie Dickins
Illustrated by Graham Philpot

THE FROG PRINCE   80

By the Brothers Grimm, retold by Susanna Davidson
Illustrated by Mike Gordon

THE DRAGON PAINTER   104

Retold by Rosie Dickins
Illustrated by John Nez

SNOW WHITE AND THE SEVEN DWARFS 128

By the Brothers Grimm, retold by Lesley Sims
Illustrated by John Joven

THE TWELVE DANCING PRINCESSES 156

By the Brothers Grimm, retold by Lara Bryan
Illustrated by Anna Luraschi

THE MAGIC WISHBONE 182

Based on a fairy tale by Charles Dickens, retold by Lara Bryan
Illustrated by Qin Leng

THE PRINCESS AND THE PEA 206

By Hans Christian Andersen, retold by Susanna Davidson
Illustrated by Mike Gordon

ALADDIN AND HIS MAGICAL LAMP 230

Retold by Katie Daynes
Illustrated by Paddy Mounter

LITTLE RED RIDING HOOD

Once there was a girl called Little Red Riding Hood. She was called that because she always wore a pretty, patterned cape with a bright red hood. She just loved the way the cape swished and swayed, as she skipped along.

One day, Little Red Riding Hood's mother gave her a pot of honey. "Will you take this to Grandma?" she asked.

Little Red Riding Hood was delighted. Grandma lived on the other side of the forest, so she could skip all the way there in her lovely red cape.

Little Red Riding Hood waved to her father as she set off. But watching from the trees was a hungry wolf. The wolf was tired of eating bugs and berries. He wanted something bigger in his belly. Something like Little Red Riding Hood...

He could have just gobbled her up there and then, but this wolf loved sneaking around, making clever traps.

Chortling and chuckling, the wolf laid
a net on the forest path. Then he hid by a
tree and waited for Little Red Riding Hood.

The wolf watched
as Little Red Riding
Hood skipped closer
and closer...and skipped
right over the net!

"Why didn't it work?"
growled the wolf.
Carefully, he prodded
the net with his paw...

...and the net
sprang up, trapping
the wolf instead.

By the time he had escaped from the net, the wolf was too tired and too hungry to make another trap. But he did have another plan. Grinning and giggling, he rushed to Grandma's house and knocked on the door.

The door opened slowly and Grandma poked her head out. "Who's there?" she croaked.

Quick as a flash, the wolf leaped from behind the door and gobbled poor Grandma up in one greedy gulp.

"Mmm," he mumbled. "That was a tasty starter. Now for the main course..."

The wolf pulled on Grandma's night clothes and jumped into her bed. His eyes twinkled and a grin spread across his face, as he heard a knock on the door. "Come in," he called out, in a croaking, wavery voice.

The door swung open and Little Red Riding Hood skipped into the cottage. "Hello Grandma," she trilled. "I've brought you some honey."

Little Red Riding Hood came closer, and her smile fell into a frown. Grandma looked...different. "Oh Grandma," she said. "What big ears you have."

"All the better to hear you with, my dear," replied the wolf.

Little Red Riding Hood edged closer still. "Oh Grandma, what big eyes you have."

"All the better to see you with," muttered the wolf.

"Oh Grandma, what big, hairy hands you have," exclaimed Little Red Riding Hood.

"All the better to hug you with," replied the wolf.

Little Red Riding
Hood stepped back,
as the wolf's grin
spread even wider.
"Um, Grandma,"
she said, "what big
TEETH you have."

"All the better
to eat you with!"
snarled the wolf.
With that, he
sprang from the bed
and swallowed Little
Red Riding Hood up
in one big bite.

The wolf had never felt so pleased with himself. His plan had worked and his belly was totally full. He lay back on Grandma's bed and fell into a deep, happy sleep.

Zzzzz...

Meanwhile, in the forest, Little Red Riding Hood's father had finished a hard morning's work, chopping down trees.

He decided to go to Grandma's house, so he could walk home with Little Red Riding Hood. "There are wolves in these woods, after all," he thought.

Little Red Riding Hood's father was in for a shock. He reached the cottage, looked through a window...and there was the wolf, with an enormous belly, fast asleep in Grandma's bed.

Little Red Riding Hood's father boiled with rage.

"Has that greedy wolf eaten Grandma and Little Red Riding Hood?" he gasped. "The villain! But maybe I can still save them."

So Little Red Riding Hood's father came up with a clever plan of his own.

With one mighty swing, he smashed open the front door of Grandma's cottage.

With a second mighty swing, he cut open the sleeping wolf's belly.

Out tumbled Grandma and Little Red Riding Hood! Little Red Riding Hood jumped into her father's arms, although Grandma looked a little shaken from her time in the wolf's tummy.

"Are you all right?" asked Little Red Riding Hood's father.

"I... I think so," Grandma gulped.

"What shall we do about the wolf?" asked Little
Red Riding Hood. "If we let him go, he might
gobble up someone else in the forest."

Now it was Grandma's turn to come up with
a brilliant plan. She told Little Red Riding Hood
to run outside and bring her some rocks.

So Little Red Riding Hood did, and rushed back
with a pile of speckled stones. Grandma asked
her to tip them into the wolf's tummy, so she did
that, too. Finally, Grandma stitched up the wolf's
tummy – and then they all dashed outside to hide,
just as the wolf began to wake.

The wolf yawned and stretched and then sat up on the bed. At first, he didn't notice anything unusual. But when he tried to stand, something rattled in his belly...the stones. Now the wolf couldn't move without them rattling.

The wolf howled so hard, it made the whole cottage shake. The stones rattled louder and louder, with each shaky step, as he trudged back into the forest. "Now I won't be able to sneak around and set traps any more," he moaned.

And the wolf never did. Instead, he went back to eating boring old bugs and berries.

As for Little Red Riding Hood, she skipped all the way home in her pretty, patterned cape.

THE ELVES AND THE SHOEMAKER

Long ago, there was an old shoemaker, whose shoes were once admired far and wide. But years of hammering heels and stitching leather had left him in agony. His back ached and his fingers throbbed. He could no longer make such wonderful shoes.

All day long, the shoemaker stood at
the entrance to his shop, watching people come
and go. In the past, his shop had been full of
customers eager to snap up his shoes. But now
no one came, and his shop sat silent and empty.

The shoemaker stared at his last scraps of leather and sighed. He had enough to make one more pair of shoes, but would anyone buy them?

The shoemaker's wife saw how upset her husband was and knew he needed rest. "Come to bed, dear," she called to him. "We can think about it again in the morning."

The shoemaker left the leather on his workbench. He knew he would soon have to close his shop forever. But the very next morning...

...there, on the shoemaker's workbench, was a brand new pair of shoes! And what stunning shoes – sleek and stylish and exquisitely stitched.

The shoemaker
put them on
display and soon a
crowd had gathered
outside his shop.

"What fabulous
footwear!" they
all agreed.

The shoemaker
sold the new shoes
the moment he
opened his shop.
Now, he could
afford leather to
make two pairs
of shoes.

That night, the shoemaker left the leather
on his workbench again and went to bed...
The next morning, there was another surprise.

Two new pairs of boots stood on the bench.
They were even more magnificent than the shoes,
with twirly patterns and pointed toes.

The first pair of shoes had sold in minutes; these
boots were so splendid that they sold in seconds.
The shoemaker and his wife were flabbergasted, but
delighted. Who was making these wonderful shoes
and boots? They had no idea who it could be or how
they were getting into the workshop. It was as if a
guardian angel were watching over them...

The strange shoe magic continued for weeks. Each night, the shoemaker left leather on his workbench and, each morning, he discovered brand new shoes. Sometimes three or four pairs appeared overnight and each time they were finer than the morning before. Some had fancy ribbons, others had elegant buckles or handsome high heels.

Word spread that the shoemaker was making
fine shoes again and customers came from far and
wide to buy them. The shoemaker was happy but,
more and more, he felt awkward about his change
of fortune. They weren't his shoes, after all.
Someone else was doing all the work – and he
wanted to know who...

So, one night,
he made a plan.
"Let's hide in the
workshop tonight,"
he told his wife.
"We can see
who comes."

That night, the
shoe shop door
opened with a creak.
The shoemaker and
his wife hid as two
shadows darted
across the golden
moonlight.

43

As the shoemaker and his wife watched, two tiny creatures in raggedy clothes sprang up onto the workbench. They were giggling and grinning and dancing and singing.

"They're ELVES!" the shoemaker's wife gasped. "All of this time, have two tiny little elves been making all those incredible boots and shoes?"

The shoemaker and his wife gazed in astonishment as the elves got to work.

Smiling and singing, the little creatures hammered heels and stitched leather...

By the first light of morning, the latest pair of shoes was finished. The cheery elves leaped from the bench and scampered away.

The shoemaker and his wife could barely believe what they had seen. But the new shoes proved it was real – and they were the finest yet.

"What magical creatures those elves are," the shoemaker's wife said. "Somehow we must repay their kindness."

The shoemaker agreed. But what could he make for an elf?

The shoemaker had an idea. For the first time in weeks, he sat at his workbench, cutting and stitching leather and cloth.

His back ached and his fingers throbbed, but he didn't give up, even as his candle burned down and his eyes stung in its flickering light.

The shoemaker left
what he had made on
the workbench for the
elves to find and went
to bed. Later that night,
the elves crept
silently into the shop...

When they saw
the shoemaker's
gifts, they squealed
with joy. "What
fantastic new suits,"
they cried in delight.
"Such terrific top
hats and tails."

The suits were finer than anything worn by dukes or lords or princes or kings. The elves danced around the workbench, gleefully singing about their magnificent new clothes.

"What happy little elves are we," one sang, "no longer workmen shall we be."

"We look so fine in our new suits," the other elf joined in, "no longer shall we stitch new boots."

Finally, they skipped out of the shoe shop and into the silvery moonlight, still singing and dancing and giggling about how handsome they both looked in their new clothes. As they ran off, one of the elves called out, "Thank you shoemaker! And goodbye!"

The shoemaker and his wife watched them disappear into the night. "Thank you too," the shoemaker whispered. Thanks to those kind little creatures, he and his wife could live comfortably for the rest of their lives.

The shoemaker and his wife never saw the elves again, or knew why the creatures had helped them. But whenever he thought about the elves, the shoemaker smiled.

He hoped they were
still singing and dancing
somewhere, in their fine
hand-stitched suits.

The Emperor and the Nightingale

Woof!
Woof!

The Emperor of China was used to getting whatever he wanted – and he wanted to fill his palace with music. He tried to train his dog to sing, but all it could do was bark.

He tied strings of silver bells onto the flowers in the palace gardens. The bells tinkled prettily in the breeze, but it wasn't a real song.

Ting!
Ting-a-ling!

"Perhaps you could send for musicians?" suggested a servant.

"No," sighed the Emperor. "I want to hear something different – something rare and exquisite..."

He leafed listlessly through his books, looking for ideas. Nothing seemed quite right, until he came to a page headed 'The Nightingale'.

It said: "The song of the nightingale is the sweetest music of all."

The Emperor sprang up. "I want a nightingale!" he told his servants. "Find one and bring it here to sing. Immediately!"

The palace servants had never heard of a
nightingale before, but they did their best.
They began by searching the gardens. They
poked through bushes and peeked under flowers,
but found only spiders and snails.

"Where is the nightingale?" they cried.
"What does it look like?"

An old gardener heard them. "Are you
looking for the nightingale?" he said.
"I can show you where she
lives. Just follow me."

Walking across a bridge, they heard
a sudden noise. **Ribbit-ribbit**!
"The nightingale!" cried the servants.

Ribbit-ribbit!

The gardener smiled. "No, that's
a frog in the lily pond," he said,
pointing to it. "The nightingale's song
is much more beautiful."

A little later, there was another noise. **Moo-ooo!**

"The nightingale!" cried the servants again.

"No, that's a cow in the meadow," said the
gardener, shaking his head and trying not to laugh.

"The nightingale's song is much more beautiful! Hush, there she is now."

There in a cherry tree was a little brown bird and she was singing...

The nightingale's song was as sweet and soft as a summer evening. The servants listened till she had finished. Then... "Little bird," they begged. "Will you sing for the Emperor in his palace?"

"My song sounds best outside, among the trees," replied the nightingale. "But I will come."

The Emperor was very surprised when the
gardener brought in a little brown bird.

"She doesn't look very special," he thought to
himself. Then the nightingale opened her beak and
sang, and he was enchanted.

"Little bird, I want you to stay and sing to me every day," he told her.

The Emperor gave the nightingale a splendid silver cage. The servants brought her everything she needed. But she missed living outside, among the trees, and her heart grew heavy.

The Emperor loved inviting people to hear the
nightingale. As her fame spread, visitors came
from far and wide.

One day, the Emperor of Japan
came. "Such sweet music,"
he said admiringly.

After the Emperor of Japan returned home, he sent the Emperor of China a gift. It arrived in a large painted box tied up with ribbon.

Eagerly the Emperor of China untied the bow and peeked inside...

"How beautiful!" he gasped.

To: the Emperor of China
Here's a prettier nightingale!
From: the Emperor of Japan

It was another nightingale – but this one was
made of glittering gold and jewels. It had a golden
key in its back and, when you turned the key,
it sang a stiff little song.

The Emperor was so entranced
by the golden bird, he didn't
notice the little brown
nightingale fly away.

The Emperor played the golden nightingale morning, noon and night. Each time, its stiff little tune sounded exactly the same.

The Emperor chuckled and clapped, delighted with his new toy. "This is truly a bird fit for an emperor," he told himself proudly.

Then one day,
instead of singing,
the golden bird went
whizz-whirr and
ker-plunk. Something
had snapped inside
and no one knew how
to fix it.

The Emperor
summoned expert
after expert.
They tutted and
muttered and
shook their heads –
but the golden bird
remained broken.

Now the Emperor begged his servants to bring back the little brown bird. But this time no one could find her, not even the gardener.

Without music, the palace felt quiet and lonely. The Emperor pined. Then, he became sick. He lay in bed, staring sadly at the broken bird. Silence and shadows surrounded him. His doctors feared he was close to death.

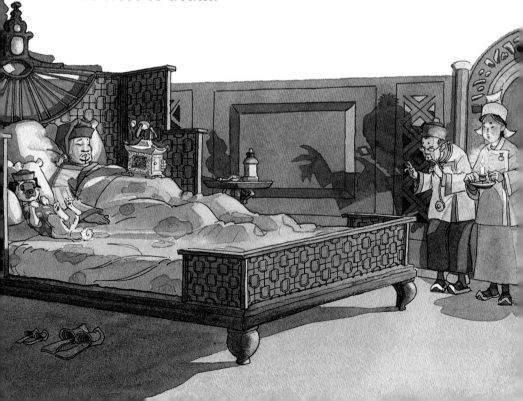

Very early one morning, the sound of birdsong
filled the air, as sweet and soft as a summer
evening... It was the real nightingale. She had
heard the Emperor was sick and she had come
back to sing for him.

She sang so sweetly that the shadows around the
Emperor seemed to fade. He smiled – and, at last,
he began to get better.

Soon the Emperor was well again. "You cured me," he told the little bird. "Thank you! Please stay with me in the palace. You can have a golden cage and all the servants you want!"

"No, thank you," trilled the nightingale, shaking her head. "You see, I prefer to live outside, among the trees." And, with that, she darted out of the window and away, into the wide blue sky.

The Emperor stared wistfully after her until she had vanished from view.

Farewell!

The Emperor missed the nightingale so much, he asked the gardener to plant a tree outside his bedroom window.

"It will remind me of her," he said.

The gardener planted a beautiful fruit tree and watered it every day. It grew and grew.

One day, the Emperor heard something fluttering in the branches. He looked out...

There were not one but
two nightingales, building
a nest in the tree! And
when they sang, everyone
in the palace smiled to
hear them – the Emperor
most of all.

THE FROG PRINCE

Princess Poppy was furious. "I won't marry Prince Humperdink, Daddy! He's smelly and smug and slimier than a frog. In fact, I'd rather eat my toenails. I'll find another prince to marry."

"You can have until tomorrow morning," said her father, the king. "But you'll never find a prince in that time."

"Just you wait," said Poppy. She picked up her golden ball and stomped into the garden.

Poppy was so cross, she
didn't see the wobbly stone.
She wibbled...she wobbled...
She slipped and fell...

...face-first into the palace pond.

SPLAT!

Her beautiful
golden ball flew
out of her hands
and plopped into
the pond. "Oh no!"
Poppy groaned. "My
birthday present
from Daddy!"

Poppy gazed into the pond, hoping to see her
ball. Instead, she came face to face with a pair
of big, bulging eyes. "Urgh!" she cried.
"How revolting! A frog."

Hello, Princess Poppy!

"I see you have lost your ball," said the frog. "Please, allow me to find it for you."

I am at your service.

"Oh," said Poppy. "Thank you."
"But you must promise me something first," said the frog.
"Anything!" cried Poppy.

"I want to live
in your palace,"
said the frog.

"I want to eat
with you, drink with
you and sleep on
your pillow."

"In your dreams,"
thought Poppy. But
out loud she said,
"I promise."

SPLISH!

The frog plunged into the water and returned, moments later, with the golden ball.

"Oh! Hooray!" shouted Poppy.

She snatched up the
ball and raced back
to the palace.

"Hey!" the frog
called after her.
"What about
your promise?"

Wait for me!

But Poppy didn't
stop. The little frog
hopped as fast as he
could, but he couldn't
catch up with Poppy.

Poppy arrived back at the palace just in time for dinner.

"There you are," said the king.

"You're late," said the queen. "Come and sit next to Prince Humperdink."

Poppy groaned as she took her place.

"I hope there's cabbage!" Prince Humperdink began, when there was a faint tapping sound.

"Is someone at the door?" asked the king.

Poppy had a sinking feeling. She rushed to the door and opened it.

"Hello again," said the frog.

"Oh no! Not you," said Poppy, and she swiftly slammed the door in his face.

"Who was that?" asked the king.

"No one," said Poppy quickly.

"I was sure I heard someone..." said Prince Humperdink. "Are you sure it was nothing?"

"Yes!" Poppy shouted.

The tapping noise came again.

"I'll ask the footman to look," said the king.

"No, Daddy, don't!" cried Poppy. "It's... a frog!"

How shocking!

How horrible!

"He rescued my golden ball from the pond and I sort of said he could stay with me," admitted Poppy.

ugh!

"Well, you must keep your promise," the king insisted. Reluctantly, Poppy opened the door. The frog shot inside.

He followed Poppy all the way back to her chair. She could hear his wet feet going splat, splat, splat on the floor behind her.

"Excuse me," said the frog, "but Princess Poppy did promise I could eat from her plate. May I sit at the table too?"

"Oh dear," said Prince Humperdink.

"Certainly not,"
snapped Poppy,
crossly.

"Don't be so rude,"
said the king. "The
frog is our guest."

"We're eating watercress soup," the king went
on. "Please, help yourself."

The frog dived into Poppy's bowl.

Ahh... This is the life.

"I don't think I'm hungry anymore," said Poppy,
as the frog slurped up the last of her soup. "Can
I go to bed early?"

"Poppy," said the king, sternly. "Remember
your manners."

The frog smiled. "What's the next course?"

The next course
was frogs' legs.

"I might skip this
one," said the frog.

Poppy didn't
usually eat frogs'
legs, but that night,
she had seconds.

"Time for bed!"
said the frog. "I can
sleep on your pillow."

"Oh no!" wailed
Poppy. "Please not."

"Poppy!" said the
king, firmly.

You can carry me on a cushion.

Poppy took a
deep breath and
stretched out her
arm. She picked
up the frog by
one foot.

"She touched him!" moaned Prince
Humperdink, and fainted.

Poppy dropped the
frog in the darkest,
most distant corner
of her room.

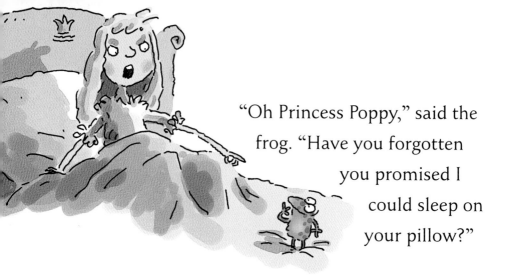

"Oh Princess Poppy," said the frog. "Have you forgotten you promised I could sleep on your pillow?"

"I've had enough!" yelled Poppy. "You're the meanest, ugliest, most horrible frog I've ever met. Mention my promise again and I'll throw you out of the window."

"Your promise!" chanted the frog.

"Ha!" said Poppy, and out he went...

There was a long
silence, followed by
a loud SPLAT.

"Oh dear!" said
Poppy, realizing
what she'd done.
"I do hope I haven't
killed him."

She raced outside.

Froggy!

Poppy picked up
the frog as gently
as she could. "Are
you all right?" she
whispered. "Are you
still alive?"

"I think so," said the frog, opening his eyes.

"I'm so glad," said Poppy, and she bent down and kissed him.

There was a loud crash of thunder followed by a shower of sparks.

The frog had vanished and in his place stood a handsome young prince.

"At last!" shouted the prince. "I'm human again. No more slimy skin, no more webbed feet, no more flies..."

What happened to you?

"A wicked witch cast a spell on me," he explained. "I could only become a human again if a princess kissed me."

"How can I make it up to you?" asked the prince.

"Well," Poppy replied. "You could marry me."

"Excuse me," said Prince Humperdink, "but Poppy is going to marry ME."

"No I'm not," said Poppy. "And Daddy did say I could find my own prince."

"That's true," sighed the king.

"In that case," said the prince, getting down on one knee...

"Princess Poppy, if you promise not to throw me out of the window again, will you marry me?"

"I will," said Princess Poppy.

And, when she grew up, that's exactly what she did.

THE DRAGON PAINTER

Zhang loved to paint. He painted lavish landscapes, with misty mountains and twisty trees. He painted bowls brimming with bright, beautiful fruit and flowers.

But his pictures of animals were the best of all.
From fluttery butterflies to fat, feathered hens,
every creature he painted trembled with life. His
birds looked as if they might fly right off the paper.
His rabbits almost twitched their noses. People
came from all over the country to admire them.

One day, Zhang was strolling through the town when he bumped into a priest. The priest seemed a little upset.

"What's the matter?" asked Zhang kindly.

"It's these pesky pigeons," the priest explained. "They built a nest in the temple and they're making a terrible mess! Just look at that statue."

Zhang looked...

Splat! Something white splattered the statue's head.

"Oh dear," said Zhang. He tugged his beard thoughtfully. Then he smiled. "I think I can help."

"Really?" cried the priest eagerly. "HOW?"

"Leave it to me," said Zhang. "Please find a ladder, while I mix some paints."

When the priest came back, Zhang was ready.
He climbed up the ladder and began to paint.
Splish, splosh! As his brush darted back and forth,
a creature took shape. It had powerful wings,
sharp, curving claws and a wicked-looking beak...

It was an eagle, swooping down to pounce on its prey! The pigeons eyed it with alarm, flapping about nervously while Zhang worked. As he added the finishing touches, they finally flew away.

"I don't think you'll be seeing that pair again," laughed Zhang, clambering back down the ladder.

"Thank you," sighed the priest.

Zhang's fame grew, until even the Emperor heard about him. The Emperor summoned Zhang to his palace.

"I have a new pavilion I want you to decorate," the Emperor told Zhang. "Can you do dragons?"

In reply, Zhang whipped out his brush and began to sketch.

Zhang planned a splendid mural with four dragons, one for each wall of the pavilion.

News of the mural spread. By the time Zhang was ready to start, a crowd had gathered to watch.

Splish, splosh! Zhang's brush darted back and
forth over the first wall, conjuring up a sleek,
serpent-like creature. It had shimmering,
pearl-white scales and magnificent whiskers.
Clouds of steam curled from its gaping mouth.

Just one thing seemed strange to the Emperor
and the watching crowd...

The pearl dragon's
eyes were blank
and empty.

Splish, splosh! On the second wall, a spiky, jade-green beast took shape. It had clutching claws and toothy jaws and a VERY pointy nose.

It was truly awe-inspiring, except for one thing...

The jade dragon's eyes were blank and empty too.

Splish, splosh! Zhang filled the
third wall with a dazzling golden
dragon. Its long, elegant body snaked
across the wall in fantastical loops and coils,
covered with gleaming spikes and scales.

It looked amazing. There was only one problem
with it...

The gold dragon's eyes were blank and empty.

Splish, splosh! The last dragon was a fabulous flame-red beast, tinged with fiery orange and brilliant yellow.

It was a masterpiece, except for one thing...

Its eyes were blank and empty too.

Zhang put down his brush and turned to the Emperor.

"It is done, Your Highness," he said, with a bow.

"What do you mean?" snapped the Emperor, scowling. "You haven't finished their eyes!"

"Um," said Zhang nervously. "I can't do that."

Don't be silly!

"Dragons are magical creatures," Zhang went
on. "If I dot in their eyes, they will come to life!"

"Piffle!" snapped the Emperor impatiently.

"I ORDER you to finish these dragons!"

Zhang had no choice. He couldn't disobey the Emperor. Reluctantly, he picked up his brush and turned back to the pearl dragon. Slowly, he dotted in the first eye...

KABOOM!

As he dotted the second eye, the sky outside
grew dark. Lightning flashed and thunder crashed,
shaking the pavilion on its foundations.

Zhang glanced nervously at the Emperor. "Your
Highness, I don't think this is a good idea."

The Emperor had barely noticed the strange change in weather. He was too busy admiring the finished dragon.

"I won't listen to silly superstitions," he scoffed. "And I certainly won't have unfinished dragons! Finish the rest immediately."

Poor Zhang had no choice.

With a trembling hand, he dotted in
the eyes of the jade dragon...

...and the gold dragon...

...and the red one.

There was a moment's pause. Then...

"Look!" gasped an onlooker, pointing. The jade dragon was blinking, as if it had just woken up. It yawned and stretched and... CRACK! Its spiky nose struck a stone pillar and snapped it.

"Watch out!" yelled someone else. The pearl dragon was slithering slowly across its wall, breathing out billowing clouds of steam. The people nearby ran for their lives.

Another bolt of lightning flashed through the sky and struck the pavilion... KER-RACK!

The lightning burned a hole right through the roof. The jade and pearl dragons stared up at it. Then they sprang off their walls and flew out of the hole together, without a backwards glance.

They soared up, up, up into the darkening sky,
until they vanished among the clouds.

"Stop them!" shouted the Emperor. But it
was too late. The dragons were gone.

Then the red and gold dragons began to stir...
Quickly, Zhang grabbed his brush and added
chains around their necks. The dragons clinked
and they clanked, but they couldn't fly away.

So the Emperor had to be content with only two dragons on his pavilion walls. But they were the most wonderful painted dragons in all of China.

And, to this day, the phrase 'dotting the eyes on a painted dragon' is used in China to mean adding the finishing touches.

SNOW WHITE AND THE SEVEN DWARFS

Sometimes, wishes are granted. Once, a queen wished all winter long for a child. The following year, she had a beautiful baby daughter, with pale skin and lips as red as holly berries.

"I'll name her Snow White," said the queen.

The king and queen were overjoyed, but their happiness turned to misery when the queen became ill. "Look after Snow White," she begged the king. "Marry again, someone loving and kind who will be a good mother."

Soon after, the
queen died. The king
was heartbroken, but
he remembered her
plea for him to find
a new wife.

Within a year, he had
married again. His new
queen was the most
beautiful woman in
the kingdom, but her
lovely face hid a cruel,
unfeeling heart.

The only person she cared about was herself. She spent hours gazing in her magic mirror, asking the same question: "Mirror, mirror, on the wall, who's the fairest of us all?"

You are, Your Majesty!

The new queen ignored Snow White completely. The king had no idea, for Snow White never told him.

Left on her own, Snow White grew up gentle, kind and loving. She also grew prettier every year.

One dreadful morning, the queen asked her mirror the familiar question: "Mirror, mirror, on the wall, who's the fairest of us all?"

To her horror, the mirror replied, "Snow White!" No matter how many times the queen asked, the answer was always the same.

The queen was FURIOUS. "Aaagh!"
she screamed, flushing red with rage.

She stormed around the palace,
kicking chairs and shouting
at the footmen.

"No one can be fairer than me,"
she snarled, jealously. "I will not have it.
I am the fairest! ME, ME, ME!"

When she had calmed down, she went to find the royal huntsman. "Take Snow White to the forest at once," she demanded, "and kill her!"

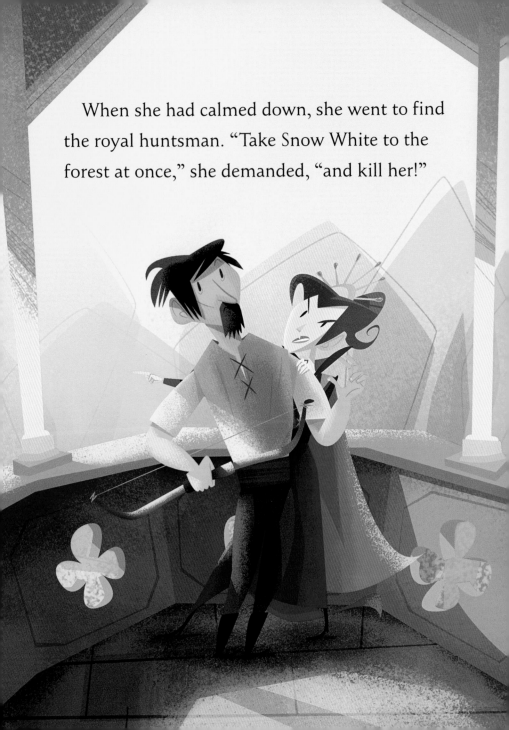

The poor huntsman didn't dare say no. Instead, he rode deep into the forest with Snow White and begged her to run away.

"The queen is wicked," he told her. "You aren't safe in the palace any more. I'm sure you will find someone to help you. Good luck!"

For a moment, Snow White stood still in shock. The forest was dark and full of strange shadows and eerie noises.

She started to run. Prickly tree branches
reached out, grasping at her as she stumbled past.
Her legs and lungs ached but still she ran.

At last, she came
to a clearing, with a
curious, red-roofed
cottage.

"Someone's home,"
she thought, seeing
smoke puffing from
the chimney.

Cautiously,
she went up and
knocked on the
small front door.

"Who could
live here?" she
murmured. "I hope
they're friendly..."

Seven dwarfs raced out, bursting with questions.
"Who are you? Where are you from? Are you
lost? Are you hungry? Come inside!"
Snow White stepped back in astonishment.

"You're just in
time for supper!"
said a dwarf.

The food grew
cold as Snow White
told them her story.

"That's terrible!"
the dwarfs chorused
when she finished.
"The queen sounds
awful. Well, you
can't go home. You
must stay here in our
cottage with us."

The next morning,
Snow White waved
them off to work.

"Be careful!" one
of the dwarfs said.
"The queen may
try to find you. Keep
a look out for her."

At that very moment,
the queen was standing
in front of her mirror. She
scowled as a misty image
of Snow White appeared.
"Snow White is still the
fairest in the land,"
the mirror announced.

Curses!

"How can the brat still be alive?" the queen screeched. "She should have perished in the forest. Well, she won't escape me a second time."

Muttering a spell, the queen transformed herself into a hunched pedlar and hobbled to the cottage in the clearing.

Snow White was entranced by the bright ribbons in the queen's basket. "Please come in," she cried.

"I have the perfect ribbon for you," the queen croaked.

She tied the sash around Snow White's waist, pulling tighter...and tighter...

Snow White
fainted and
collapsed on
the floor – and
there she stayed
until the dwarfs
discovered her.

"That old
woman was
the evil queen,"
one said, after
they had untied
the ribbon and
brought her a cup
of hot cocoa.

The dwarfs didn't want to leave Snow White alone the next morning. "Be extra careful!" they begged. "Don't let ANYONE into the cottage!"

"I won't!" Snow White promised.

Later that day, she was in the garden when a friendly girl came by.

"Would you like a glittery comb?" the girl asked. "It will look so pretty in your hair."

Snow White took it without thinking.

"Ha! Ha!" cackled a voice as Snow White fell to the ground. The little girl turned into the villainous queen, who did a gleeful dance before racing back to the palace.

"That dreadful queen!" said the dwarfs, snatching the comb from Snow White. "You'd better stay indoors tomorrow."

The queen was not pleased when her mirror sang, "Snow White is still the fairest!" But she refused to give up.

With a cunning sneer, she made a poisoned apple. It looked like the most delicious apple in the world. No one who saw it would be able to resist.

In a third disguise, she returned to the cottage and called hello through the open window.

"I can't come out!" said Snow White.

"You don't have to," said the queen, showing her the shiny red apple.

Snow White couldn't help it. She reached
through the window for the apple and took a juicy,
crunchy bite.

The poison worked in an instant. She slumped
to the ground and lay perfectly still. This time, not
even the dwarfs could save her.

"Hurray!" shouted the queen. "I'm the fairest of them all – for good." She ran home in excitement, eager to hear her mirror tell her, once again, how beautiful she was.

The dwarfs couldn't bear to bury Snow White, so they laid her in a glass case outside the cottage.

After a year and a day, a prince rode by. Snow White looked as if she were simply asleep. He took one glance at her and fell in love.

He leaped from his horse, opened the case and scooped Snow White into his arms. The piece of apple flew from her mouth.

"Oh!" she said, waking up. "Thank you for rescuing me," she added, as he carried her into the cottage.

The prince took Snow White to his kingdom far beyond the forest, where the queen could never find her. There they were married...and all seven dwarfs carried her train.

THE TWELVE DANCING PRINCESSES

There were once twelve sisters named Anna, Bella, Carla, Dora, Emma, Freya, Georgia, Hanna, Isla, Jemma, Kenza and the littlest one, Liz. They were princesses and they all lived in a castle with their grumpy dad, the king.

The king didn't approve of the
princesses having fun, and he especially
didn't like them dancing.

They twirled and
whirled to any tune
they heard. The more
they danced, the crosser
the king became.

One day, the king decided that he'd had enough. "There shall be no more hip wiggling or shoulder jiggling in my palace," he declared.

Every night, he locked all twelve princesses up in the tallest tower and dragged away the key. "That should stop them from dancing anywhere else," he thought.

It didn't. Every morning, the maid found twelve pairs of worn out dancing slippers in the princesses' tower.

When she showed the king, he spilled his hot chocolate with rage.

"Tell me where you go each night!" the king demanded, but the princesses wouldn't say a word.

"There's only one way to stop this," the king decided. "I will hold a royal competition. Whoever solves the mystery can marry one of the girls."

Posters went up throughout the land.

Brave Prince Henry was the first man to take up the king's challenge.

"I hope you read the small print," said the king. "Fail and it's off with your head!"

Before Prince Henry could change his mind, he was marched to the tower to begin.

Night fell... Princess
Emma came out of the
princesses' room with
a cup of steaming,
fragrant tea.

"Welcome to our
tower," she smiled.

Prince Henry drank the tea and his eyelids started drooping. Within minutes, he was snoring loudly. He slept deeply for the rest of the night.

Off with his head!

The next morning, the princesses' shoes were all worn out again. Prince Henry had failed. As the guards dragged him off to the dungeons, a whistle came from the passageway.

A young man and
his dog strolled in.

"Hello, Sire," he
said to the king. "I am
Milo, the magician,
and this is my trusty
dog, Moll. If I solve the
mystery, will you spare
Prince Henry's life?"

The king had seen
sparks coming from
Milo's bag.

"Very well," he
said nervously. "But
if you fail, both your
heads will roll!"

Milo was taken to the tower to start his watch.
This time, as night fell, Princess Anna came out
with a cup of steaming tea.

"Welcome to our tower," Anna smiled.

"He looks nice," Liz thought, as Milo accepted
the drink. "It's a shame he might lose his head."

Milo knew better
than to drink the
tea. When the sisters
weren't looking, he
poured it into Moll's
bowl. Moll gave a
yelp of delight. She
loved tea.

Some time later,
when Anna came to
check on him, Milo
pretended to be fast,
fast asleep.

She crept back to
the other princesses.

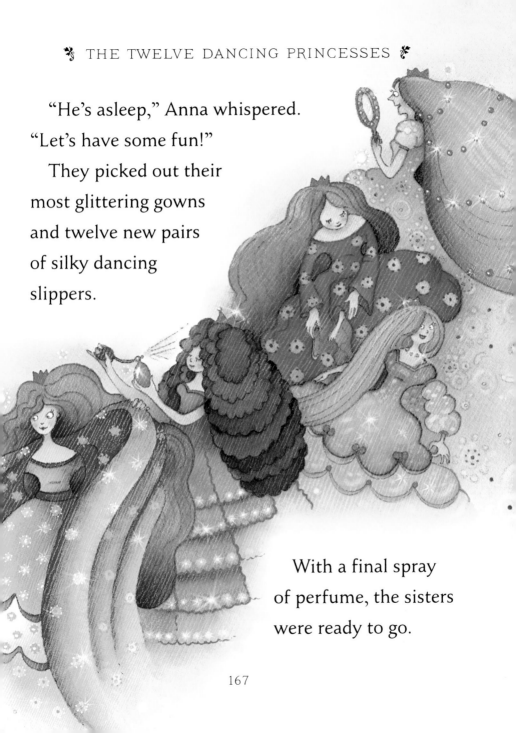

"He's asleep," Anna whispered.
"Let's have some fun!"

They picked out their
most glittering gowns
and twelve new pairs
of silky dancing
slippers.

With a final spray
of perfume, the sisters
were ready to go.

Emma rolled back the rug by her
bed, pulled up a secret trap door
and beckoned the others over.

One by one, the sisters
climbed in.

Milo peered into the
room just as the last
princess disappeared
down a flight of steps.

He waited until the
sound of their footsteps
had faded away before
following them down.

Milo looked around.
He was in a dank,
dimly-lit tunnel.

"Time for some magic,"
he thought. A thick cloak
appeared out of thin air.
He shrugged it on,
clicked his fingers...
and disappeared!

Moving swiftly, he soon caught up with the sisters.

"This is going
to be easier than
I expected," Milo
thought, as he
followed the princesses
along the tunnel. Just
then, he tripped and
stepped on Liz's
trailing scarf.

Startled, Liz
turned around.
There was no
one there.

"Someone's
behind us,"
she told Isla.

"Don't be
silly," Isla said.

Look!

Finally, they came to the end of the tunnel and Milo saw a row of astonishing trees.

Some gleamed with golden leaves...

...some sparkled with silver...

...and some seemed to be sprinkled with diamonds.

Even Milo, a magician, was impressed, and snapped off a twig from each tree. What kind of place was this?

He trailed the princesses to the edge of a shimmering lake. A candlelit castle twinkled invitingly from an island in the middle of the water.

Twelve boats with twelve
princes were waiting to carry
the princesses to the castle.

Tucking the branches under his
cloak, Milo sneaked onto Liz's boat.

Over on the island, a band had already struck up. Leaping onto the shore, the princesses shook out their dresses and began to dance under the starlit sky.

They danced through the
night, never pausing to rest
their aching feet.

Only when the sun rose, did they stop dancing and limp back to the boats for home.

Liz looked worried. They had danced the night away and now Milo's head was in danger.

Once the princesses were all back in their beds, Milo hurried to the king's study.

Waving the glittering branches, he explained what he had seen.

"Is this all a tall tale just to save your head?" the king said.

"Go and ask the princesses," Milo replied.

The king called for his eldest daughter, Anna. When she saw the branches in his hand, she blushed bright red. The king took one look at her face, and knew that Milo had been telling the truth.

"Why didn't you tell me what you were up to each night?" he asked.

"We just wanted to dance, and we knew you'd be so cross!" Anna said.

Back in the tower, the sisters
sobbed as they learned that their
secret had been discovered.

This is the worst
day of my life!

"We'll never be allowed to dance again," they
wailed. Liz sneaked out of the tower and rushed to
her father's study.

"Is Milo safe?" Liz begged, as she burst in.
"See for yourself, my dear," said the king.
Milo's head was still firmly on his neck.

Beaming, he stepped forward and
took Liz's hands. "Would you
give me the pleasure..."
"Yes please!" said Liz.

The next day, they were married. When the king saw how happy they were, he forgot his grumpiness.

"I only wish I could dance to celebrate your wedding," he said.

"We'll teach you. It's easy," Liz promised.

"In that case," cried the king, "lead me to the ballroom!"

THE MAGIC WISHBONE

Once upon a time, there was a king and queen who had nineteen children. They were royal, but very poor. They scrimped and saved but still they barely had enough money to get by.

Their eldest daughter, Alice, helped in every way she could. While her parents fretted, she looked after her brothers and sisters. They were all so busy playing games and getting into scrapes that they didn't notice how chilly the palace was.

On Alice's birthday, the king went out to buy a chicken for supper. He was leaving the shop when a silver-haired lady appeared in front of him. "Hello there, I'm Fairy Grandmarina," she said.

F-fairy who?

"I'm Alice's fairy godmother. Tonight, Alice will find a magic wishbone in her chicken. Tell her to wash it, rub it and polish it, until it shines like a—"

"How is it a magic wishbone?" the king interrupted.

"Tsst, grown ups are always so impatient. Just listen and let me explain. It will make one wish come true, provided Alice makes her wish at the RIGHT time." And before the king could ask anything else, the fairy flicked her fan and vanished.

That evening, Alice
found a wishbone
on her plate, so
the king told
her what
the fairy
had said.

Alice took
care to wash it,
rub it and polish it until it shone.

The next morning,
the queen woke up
feeling so ill, she could
not get out of bed.

Worried, Alice
thought about using
her wishbone.

Instead, she decided to
take some medicine to her
royal Mama...

...make some soup...

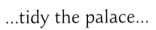

...tidy the palace...

...and play
with her brothers
and sisters.

The king watched Alice bustling about and scratched his head.

"Alice," he said, "where's the magic wishbone?"

"In my pocket, Papa."

"I thought you'd lost it?"

"Oh no, Papa."

"Or forgotten it?"

"No indeed, Papa."

The king sighed and left the room.

Ow!

That afternoon, while playing in the garden, Prince Oliver tripped and cut his hand. He yelled and yelled as his hand bled everywhere.

Alice scooped him up, cleaned the wound and patched it up. "There, there, all better," she said.

When she had
finished, Prince
Oliver had a
handsome sling.
The king, looking
through the door,
saw the bandages
and frowned.

"Alice, what have you been doing?" he asked.

"Snipping and stitching, Papa."

"Where's the magic wishbone?"

"In my pocket, Papa."

"I thought you'd lost it?"

"Oh no, Papa."

"Or forgotten it?"

"No indeed, Papa,"
said Alice, skipping off
to check on her Mama.

The next day, baby Lucy fell off her rocking horse and bumped her bottom. She howled and howled and her bottom throbbed and throbbed.

Alice rushed to the rescue. "Oh Lucy, not you too? Everyone's taking tumbles these days. Let's see if we can find something to cheer us all up."

The princes and princesses trooped into the
kitchen where Alice made them cooks' hats out of
paper and gave them each a wooden spoon.

"Let's make a cake for Mama!" she cried.

They whisked together the last of the butter,
eggs, flour and sugar, filled a tin and popped it
into the oven.

"What a mess we've made," said Alice.

After they'd cleared up, and taken some cake to the queen, the princes and princesses started a noisy pillow fight. They found the king in the throne room, surrounded by bills, looking sad.

"Alice, what have you been doing?" he said.

"Cooking and cleaning, Papa."

"Where's the magic wishbone?"

"In my pocket, Papa."

"I thought you'd lost it?"

"Oh no, Papa."

"Or forgotten it?"

"No indeed, Papa."

At this, the king's bottom lip wobbled and he burst into tears.

"Oh Papa, what's the matter?" Alice cried.

"We are so poor, I think we will have to sell the palace," said the king, throwing bills into the air.

"Is there no more money?" Alice asked.

"None at all."

"And is there any way of making more?"

"No. I have tried and tried."

"It looks as if there really is no other way.
It might be time to ask for some help," said Alice.

She took the magic wishbone from her pocket.
The princes and princesses drew nearer to watch.
The king stood still, holding his breath.

"Let's see what happens," Alice said.

She held the bone up and it shone like the sun, dazzling them all. Alice closed her eyes. She could hear her Mama coughing upstairs, her Papa sniffing next to her and her brothers and sisters shivering in the unheated room.

She made a wish.

At once, gold coins
came rattling down the
chimney and pouring into the
empty fireplace. The children tried to catch the
coins as they bounced into the room.

Suddenly, Fairy Grandmarina swooshed into the
room on a cloud of pink beating wings.

"Hello there, Alice," she said, waving.

Alice could not believe her eyes.

"The wishbone worked!" she cried.

"Do you see now why Alice didn't use the wishbone sooner?" the fairy said to the king.

The king nodded, open-mouthed.

"Well, this is just the beginning," the fairy said, smiling happily.

Fairy Grandmarina waved her fan and the
queen appeared, well again. A second wave and
the family looked down to see they were dressed
in beautiful new clothes.

"Now we just need a prince for our princess!"
she said. She swished her fan and a prince
appeared. He gazed adoringly at Alice.

"And now my dears," the fairy said, "it is time for a party." With a final flourish of her fan, she conjured up a glorious feast with roasts and pies, every sort of cake and strawberry ice cream too.

"You will all live happily ever afterwards," the fairy promised, "with no money worries and far fewer tumbles and scrapes."

"Hip, hip, hurrah!" they all cheered.

"The wishbone has worked its magic," the fairy finished. She tossed it into the fireplace, where it burst into flames.

Fairy Grandmarina was never seen again, but the fire burned merrily through the whole of the winter. It only died away with the first hints of spring.

THE PRINCESS AND THE PEA

Prince Patrick wanted to marry a princess.
But he didn't want just any old princess.
He wanted a REAL one. And not one of the
local princesses would do.

"What's the matter with them?" asked the king. "Are they too old? Too tall? Too hairy?"

"I just can't be sure they're real," sighed Prince Patrick. "I'll have to find one for myself."

"You must do whatever you want, darling," said the queen, who spoiled him rotten.

The next day
Prince Patrick set
out to travel the
world, in search of
a real princess.

He took with him twelve suitcases, ten pairs of
shoes, a spare crown and his cousin, Fred.

They hadn't gone far when they heard a loud
sneeze from under the seat.

It's Peg, the palace maid!

"What are you doing here?" asked the prince.

"I want to see the world," said Peg.

"Well, you can't come with us," said Fred. "This is a boys-only adventure."

"We're not turning back now," said the prince. "First stop is the wicked witch's hut..."

"The witch is my best hope," the prince went on. "She'll know how to find a real princess."

"Peg, you stay in the coach. This could be dangerous. Fred and I will meet the witch." The prince knocked on the witch's door.

There was no answer.

"Looks like no one's in. We'll have to go," said Fred.

"She must be in," said the prince and he bent down to peer through the keyhole.

A large green
eye stared back.
Prince Patrick let
out a loud scream.

Aaaargh!

The witch opened the door. "Did I scare you?"
she chuckled. "I'm so sorry. You can't be too
careful these days. Come inside and have some
homemade soup."

You're not
scary at all!

She's looks
scary
to me.

"I've come to ask for your help," said Prince Patrick. "I want to find a real princess."

"They're very rare," said the witch, "and it's hard to spot a fake one. But there is a test you can do. Oh yes, here we are... A real princess must have boiled brains, rotten beans and cat spit."

That doesn't sound very princessy!

"Oops. That's a recipe for soup. This is it..."

The real princess test

[A] real princess must possess...

1. Politeness to one and all

2. Kindness to rich and poor

3. Very sensitive skin

"Sensitive skin?" asked Prince Patrick.

"A real princess," explained the witch, "has such tender skin she can feel a pea under twenty mattresses."

"Do stay for lunch," added the witch. "My soup's almost ready. And bring in that poor girl from outside."

Now I can find a REAL princess.

Peg had three bowlfuls of soup, just to be polite. Afterwards, she felt rather sick.

I poured mine into a plant pot.

"Where are we going next?" asked Fred, as they climbed back into the carriage.

"Now I have the witch's test, I can finally find a real princess," said the prince. "We're off to meet Princess Prunella. Check the map, Fred."

Princess Prunella was very excited to see the prince. She raced over the bridge, dragging Prince Patrick with her. "Hurry! Hurry!" she called to the servants.

"I want you to prepare the best bedchambers for Prince Patrick and Fred."

"Excuse me," said Peg. "Where am I to sleep?"

"Maids belong in the attic!" said the princess, haughtily.

Peg went to her room. It was cold and damp and full of mice. "The prince can't marry her," thought Peg. Meanwhile...

Hello my princey!

Prince Patrick looked
around the dining room.
"Where's Peg?" he asked
Princess Prunella.

"Your beastly
little maid? You can't expect ME to bother
with HER."

"We're leaving," said the prince. "You've failed
the first real princess test. Real princesses are polite
to everyone, and you've just been
rude to Peg."

Next up was
Princess Pavlova.
She greeted them
all very politely.

"But I must
see if she's kind,"
thought the prince.
"I know! I'll dress
up as a beggar..."

First, he tried out
his disguise on Peg.

Have you any food
for me?

Of course. Please,
have my apple.

Prince Patrick rushed to the castle and knocked on the door. A servant answered.

"Is someone there?" called Princess Pavlova.

"It's a beggar, Your Highness."

"Yuck. Don't let him in."

"She's not a real princess either," Prince Patrick realized. "A real princess is polite and kind – even to beggars."

"I give up," said the prince. "I don't think there's a real princess anywhere."

They rode home. Everyone was glum, even the horses. The coach arrived back at the palace just in time. A huge storm was brewing.

Peg was sent straight to the kitchens in disgrace.

But then came a knock at the castle door. A beautiful princess entered, shaking with cold.

"I'm so sorry to trouble you," she said. "My coach has broken down. Please, may I stay?"

"She acts like a real princess," thought the prince. "But I must be sure she's REAL..."

"Of course you can stay!" cried the prince. He asked the servants to prepare the princess's bedroom. "I want twenty mattresses on the bed," he ordered, "and a pea at the very bottom."

A maid showed the princess to her bedroom. She was rather surprised.

It's very high...

Peg didn't get to bed that night. She had to wash all the dishes.

"How did you sleep?" asked the prince at breakfast the next morning.

"Like a baby," replied the princess. "I loved all those mattresses."

Prince Patrick sighed. "A real princess would have felt that pea," he thought. And he waved goodbye to the princess as soon as breakfast was over.

It was Peg's
job to clean
the princess's
bedroom. But
she was so tired
that, after climbing the
ladder to the top of the
mattresses, she fell fast
asleep. An hour
later, she woke
with a start.

"Ow! There's
something lumpy in
this bed!" she cried.
"I'm getting down."
But, as she leaned
over, she knocked
the ladder.

It clattered to the ground. "Drat," said Peg. Then, "Help!" she shouted. "I'm stuck. Please... someone, HELP!"

Everyone came running. "What are you doing up there?" asked Prince Patrick.

"I was so tired, I fell asleep," said Peg. "But there's something horribly hard in this bed."

The prince gasped. "You were polite to the witch, kind to a beggar and you felt the pea!"

You're a REAL princess!

He raced up the ladder. "Peg, will you marry me?" he asked.

A maid!

But a princess at heart!

"Yes, I'll marry you!" said Peg, and everyone
cheered. So Prince Patrick finally married his
real princess. He put the pea in a glass case for
everyone to see. It may still be there today...

ALADDIN AND HIS MAGICAL LAMP

In the ancient city of Baghdad, there lived a poor boy named Aladdin. He shared a small, cramped apartment with his hard-working mother and together they had barely enough money to live.

"One day my luck will change," Aladdin told himself, as he folded yet another shirt to sell.

And, one day, it did.

An evil magician arrived in the city and spotted Aladdin hard at work. "Just the boy I need..." he muttered to himself.

He approached
Aladdin, slyly. "My
dear boy!" he cried.
"I'm your Uncle
Abanazar, your dead
father's long-lost
brother!"

Aladdin didn't
know he had an
uncle, but he was
delighted to skip
work and follow
Abanazar on a
mystery tour into
the countryside.

Hours later,
deep in a
forest glade,
Abanazar
lit a fire and
sprinkled some
magic dust on it.

With a tiny
puff of smoke,
a trapdoor
appeared.

"Go inside,"
ordered Abanzar.
"I need you to
find the golden
lamp and bring
it to me."

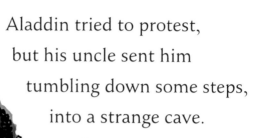

Aladdin tried to protest,
but his uncle sent him
tumbling down some steps,
into a strange cave.
"I only want the lamp.
Touch nothing else,"
ordered Abanazar.

Aladdin found the lamp, along with a rusty old
ring. Then he noticed trees full of weird, glittering
fruit. Curious, he picked a large handful.

When Aladdin finally
reached the steps,
Abanazar saw the
fruit and was
furious.

"How dare you
disobey me!" he
yelled. And, with a
loud BANG, he slammed the trapdoor shut.

Aladdin was left alone. He clasped his
hands in despair, accidentally rubbing the
old ring, and whooosh! A genie appeared.

"What is your wish?" asked the genie.

"To get home!" Aladdin cried.

In a blink, Aladdin was home. He told his mother
the mysterious tale and showed her his treasures.
"Ooh, I'll give this old lamp a polish.
Maybe we can sell it," she said.
One rub later and whoosh!
A huge genie appeared.
"What is your wish?"
he boomed.

"Um, some money to go shopping please?" asked Aladdin's mother, cautiously.

Soon, Aladdin was browsing the market with a handful of shiny coins. A large crowd had gathered to hear an important announcement from a royal servant.

"The Sultan's daughter, Princess Badra, will be visiting the public baths this afternoon," he proclaimed. "Everyone else must stay at home."

"The princess?" thought Aladdin. "I wonder what's so special about her." He decided to find out. While everyone else was at home, Aladdin crept to the baths. He peeked inside...

...and fell in love at first sight.

He floated home, starry eyed. "Mother!" he called. "I MUST marry the princess."

His mother laughed at first, until she realized he was serious.

"I'll take her father a present," she said. "Find me those glittering fruits."

The Sultan's eyes nearly popped out of his head when he saw them.

"What fabulous jewels!" he cried.

They are exquisite!

"Your son must be very wealthy indeed," said the Sultan. "If he can bring me more jewels, then he may definitely marry my daughter!"

Aladdin's mother hurried home with the news. "Don't get too excited," she warned, as Aladdin leaped for joy. "I'm not sure we can trust that Sultan..."

Sure enough, the following week there came another royal announcement. "Princess Badra is to marry Asim, the richest man in town, in two days."

Aladdin was inconsolable. Then he remembered the genie of the lamp.

No time to lose!

The night before her wedding, the genie whisked Princess Badra away to meet Aladdin.

"Don't be scared," said Aladdin, gently.

Badra had never met anyone so interesting. They talked until dawn and watched the sun rise together, before Aladdin walked Badra home.

Meanwhile, the genie gave Asim a nightmare he would never forget.

At breakfast, Badra looked miserable about marrying Asim – and Asim looked terrified.

"I'm s-sorry," he trembled. "I c-can't marry the princess. My dream said I'd turn into a frog!"

Ribbit ribbit!

Having prevented one wedding, the genie set about arranging another and conjured up a dazzling procession. "The Sultan did say he wanted more jewels..." he chuckled.

By mid-morning, forty golden plates piled with sparkling jewels were on their way to the Sultan's palace.

"NOW may my son marry your daughter?"
Aladdin's mother asked the Sultan.

The Sultan was speechless. "He may," he said at
last. "But first he must build her a palace."

Aladdin started work on the palace immediately. Or rather, he gave the genie a very long list of building instructions.

The genie let out a heavy sigh. It was going to be a busy day.

Golden domes, palm trees, ornate windows...

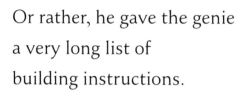

Together, Aladdin and Badra planned a sumptuous wedding. Aladdin didn't mention the genie to Badra. He wanted her to think that he was from a rich family.

As soon as the last stone of the palace was in place, the celebrations began.

Perhaps Aladdin should have had a quieter wedding. Then the evil magician wouldn't have come to see what all the fuss was about...

"The boy from the cave!" Abanazar exclaimed. "He must have escaped with the magic lamp."

A week later, Abanazar waited until Aladdin had gone out, then he strolled past the princess in her palace.

New lamps for old...

He pretended to be a street trader, exchanging new lamps for old ones.

"That sounds like a good deal," thought Badra, and she handed over Aladdin's old lamp.

"Ha, ha!" crowed Abanazar, giving the lamp a rub. Whoosh!

"Now you must obey ME," he told the genie, quickly making his first wish. "Whisk me, the princess and her palace to a desert far away."

AND DO IT IMMEDIATELY!

The Sultan got the shock of his life when he
looked out of his window.

"Find my daughter, at once!"
he screamed at Aladdin.

Aladdin felt completely
helpless without the lamp...
until he remembered the genie
of the ring.

"Please take me to
Badra," he begged.

Aladdin!
Help me.

A second later,
Aladdin was in the
desert, gazing up at
his worried wife.

"An evil magician
has trapped me
in our palace,"
she cried.

"My so-called uncle!" exclaimed Aladdin. "He's too powerful while he has the lamp..." he went on, thoughtfully. "I know. Offer to prepare him a meal, then put some sleeping powder in his drink. Once he's asleep, you can take the lamp and escape."

Badra followed Aladdin's advice. As Abanazar began to snore, she quickly found the lamp and raced to Aladdin, waiting at the palace gates.

"I'm sorry," said Badra. "I didn't realize the lamp was so important."

"It's my fault," Aladdin reassured her. "I should have told you. I didn't want you to know that I have no riches of my own. They've all been magicked up by a genie."

"I loved you even before I knew you were rich!" said Badra. "It's only my father who's obsessed with money."

Aladdin rubbed the lamp and with a wish they were back in Baghdad. "I don't think we need you any more," Aladdin said to the genie. "Just one last wish though..."

The genie eyed Aladdin suspiciously.

"Please rid us of that evil magician."

"With pleasure!" replied the genie.

And that was the last they saw of Abanazar – or the genie.

After that, Aladdin and Badra lived very happily in their palace. When Badra's father died, Aladdin became the Sultan of Baghdad. And, a few years later, Aladdin's mother became a grandmother.

As for the ring and the lamp? They are still lying somewhere, waiting to be discovered.

Edited by Lesley Sims
Cover illustration: Lorena Alvarez
Digital imaging: Nick Wakeford and John Russell